Wings

of

Morning

Katharine Eliska Kimbriel

Wings of Morning
Katharine Eliska Kimbriel
First Edition Copyright © Katharine Eliska Kimbriel, 2005
Secpmd Edition Copyright © Katharine Eliska Kimbriel, 2016

Published by Yard Dog Press at Kindle / Create Space

ISBN 978-1-937105-91-4
Wings of Morning
Secpmd Edition Copyright © Katharine Eliska Kimbriel, 2016

Yard Dog Press
710 W. Redbud Lane
Alma, AR 72921-7247

http://www.yarddogpress.com

Edited by Selina Rosen
Copy Editor James K. Burk
Technical Editor Lynn Rosen
Cover art by Christopher Hershberger

Second Print Edition June, 2016
Printed in the United States of America
0 9 8 7 6 5 4 3 2 1

Dedication

This one's for Whit.

Table of Contents

Intro for Wings

This story was originally a tale of the *future*, in its first incarnation. When I mentally planned the tale, Vietnam was a mess, India and Pakistan were threatening each other, China had atomic weapons, Korea was building the second-largest land army in the world...and Hopi oral tradition, like other native mythologies, was prophesying the end of the world. But in the Hopi histories, worlds end—and worlds begin.

I dreamt of destruction, of a thin man with sunken features chiseling away at petroglyphs on a wall. The symbols were in vertical rows, as if they were a language, and I was filled with grief at their loss.

When Roger Zelazny died, I had to honor him in the language he had taught me, the language where story trickles out of myth, and legends are born under modern skies. Unlike some writers, I don't take many notes. I read, I think...I let my subconscious weigh bits and pieces. Finally, a new form takes shape.

This tale is now a story of the *near future*. Laptops are now powerful enough to print schematics, fabrics increase in versatility and more nations join the "We have nukes, too" club. We're not quite a NorAmerican Forces, but we're already a continental trading bloc. It's only a matter of time.

Are we learning anything from history? Some of us are. Can we hold the center long enough for humanity to grow beyond its madness? I hope so. If we can't, I pray there are people like Brenna and David who survive the fireworks, and remember what must not be forgotten.

I, at least, will struggle to remember.

If I Take the Wings of Morning

They were early; the air shuttle had beaten even the sun to Third Mesa. Blue-gray sky was giving way to growing eastern light as the transport hatch swung open with a harsh metallic crack. Within the frame of rock and dry scrub before her, Brenna saw a jackrabbit shocked out of hiding; it plunged off into the brush, its white tail a flag of warning.

"Any regrets, woman?"

Duncan's choice of words caused her to tense; then she realized he had spoken in the tongue of her childhood, and her spine relaxed.

"Nay, Duncan," she answered in the same pidgin, conscious of the soldier behind them. "I told you I'd take this job for you, and neither drought nor death will sway me." Laying a delicate hand upon his gnarled arm, she added: "Just because the military is here doesn't mean it wasn't an accident."

The old man grunted, stepping heavily from the open hatchway into the dirt. "The problem with you, niece, is that you have no fear." Turning, he accepted the flight packs the young man held out to him.

Smiling thinly, Brenna shook back her dark hair, trying to capture its fullness in a thong. Even lifted from her neck, it drew a line of warmth where it lay curling down her spine. "Ah, no, Duncan," she protested, this time in English. "I'm a Kelt, and we Kelts fear only one thing–that someday the sky will fall upon us. Are we expecting thunderstorms?"

"The Hopi are," their pilot offered. Gesturing toward the foot of the mesa, he continued: "The caves are there, and Colonel Asbin's headquarters over by the road."

Brenna's gaze traveled up the sheer, rocky side of Third Mesa, up into the cloudless sky. Expecting rain? No one bothered to predict weather up here, much less control it. She saw movement on the cliff; a farmer or shepherd descending a footpath, ready for a day's work in the valley.

"*Hopi sinom,*" Duncan said softly, setting the bags at her feet.

"Are they really the little people of peace?" Brenna asked, directing her words to no one in particular.

The pilot shrugged. "Other than making site workers nervous with portents of doom, they have been harmless enough. At least they haven't firebombed this dig like the Navajos did the other." A vague gesture indicated that the aging polychrome cube closest to the cliff would be theirs.

Seizing the stiff strap, Brenna tossed her pack over one shoulder. Duncan's bad back meant they traveled light–very light, this trip. *I need no references, I know it blindfolded*, he had told her back in Flagstaff. Studying her uncle's bent, wiry frame, Brenna hoped so. The elderly man had been desperate for one last visit to the Hopi, and Brenna had wanted a light load after two years away from anthropology. This desolate slice of North America was as good a place as any.

From shadow to sun and then shadow again. The star was edging past the horizon, glittering like molten gold. It would be a standard August day, hot and dry. The green of the tiny farm plots was startling against the dust. *How long?* she wondered. A village had existed on this site since 1150 AD, Oraivi the oldest continuously occupied settlement on the continent. How much had the weather changed in that time?

"I recognize that lass," Duncan murmured suddenly, nodding toward the smiling, sloe-eyed girl who had just left one of the foam sleeping cubes. "Ling A-Ttavitt, a decent site artist. You glance inside, eh?" Straightening, the man moved agilely to greet the student, giving Brenna some of the solitude she needed for her observations. Grateful for his perception, Brenna moved quickly toward the slit in the rock.

It was up a wash of stone; sentries stood at the bottom. Since Brenna no longer feared a military presence, she had not questioned the visible guardians of the dig. Duncan's reasoning had been more direct–he wanted no aggravation this trip.

Brenna climbed the rubble handily, dropping her bag before the opening. Slipping into the narrow crevice, she was momentarily startled by illuminaries blazing at her entrance.

A short, winding corridor leading to a wide chamber...the silence was profound. Sifted dirt lay deep at her feet, mute evidence that neither animal nor water had invaded this sanctuary in centuries. *How old?* Perhaps too old for the memory of the tribe who lived above it, but it would be worth a try. She had no doubt Strand had not bothered to question the elders–he had been interested only in immutable history. A living tradition would have threatened him.

Both pictographs and petroglyphs covered the walls of the chamber, the former in several colors, the latter deeply incised. Nodding absently, Brenna's eyes focused momentarily on the beckoning darkness beyond. She lowered herself onto a rock near the center of the grotto, studying the paintings in the indirect light. The color was still strong, indicating that the cave had been sealed a long time.

They were interconnected, a story.... Curiosity quivered within her; it had been a long time since she had felt any interest in her work. Brenna waited, listening for an inner voice. Nothing. It had been over two years since she had courted the ghosts of the past. Had her gift faded beyond recall? Was she finally–

A tendril touched her, like a finger of cold air. She shivered, oblivious to the rising temperature outside. There was something.... Brenna stood, moving instinctively toward the inner corridor.

"It dead-ends." A-Ttavitt's voice was loud in the stillness, her presence startling Brenna.

Masking sudden annoyance, Brenna said coolly: "There's been shift, I can see some kind of small opening."

"Where Dr. Strand was injured." Brenna's head snapped around at her words. "It triggered the heart attack."

The feeling grew, drawing her. Not new ghosts; old ones. There was reverence, gentleness...the same uneasy sensation that touched her in cathedrals. Whirling abruptly, rejecting the thought, she rushed back down the corridor. A-Ttavitt hesitantly followed.

Duncan was waiting for them at the foot of the wash. "Ready for the mesa?" he asked, pausing to wipe sweat from his forehead with a bright red bandanna.

"Yes, old man, lead on and speak," she replied in the home tongue, slipping an arm around him as they walked. Ling's face was a study in Asian neutrality, hiding curiosity or confusion within.

"We came to this quickly," Duncan observed in the same speech. In their years of working together, a language of privacy had evolved– a mixture of Gaelic, Cymric, and smatterings of anything else convenient. But they normally did not use it in the presence of others.

"This one may be hard to shake," she murmured, and then turned to Ling, who had moved up on her left. "Forgive me, Ms. A-Ttavitt, but I wanted to tell him of the pictographs, and English is sometimes a poor language for vivid description."

"Of course," Ling said politely. Only her eyes held expression; they were wary.

Duncan stopped walking. "Ling, there is no need to escort us, I haven't forgotten the way into Oraivi. Why don't you gather up all the disks on the dig, so we can examine them this afternoon. I know how they wander from the boxes." The frail woman was clearly relieved to be dismissed, and with a quick smile hurried back toward one of the cubes.

"Why her distress?" Brenna asked in home-speech.

"She is afraid of the Hopi. The commander on the dig, Colonel Asbin, has been spreading all kinds of rumors, including that Strand was murdered by the very people who called him in." Duncan placed his feet carefully as they continued up the dusty road.

"Any truth to the rumors?"

That slight shrug again, Duncan's way of indicating that they should mind their own business. "Was Strand a healthy man? Of his old students, you probably knew him best."

"A heart condition, completely controlled by medication. He was a tough old goat." She smiled to keep up the premise of their discussion. There might be no monitoring devices on the path, but it would be simple to watch their ascent.

"We are supposed to be discussing pictographs. What do you think of them?"

"From what immediately rose out of the memory tapes, I would say Hopi or pre-Hopi," she responded.

"Humph. Memory tapes. They cannot be relied on. Feel anything?" This was asked intently; he knew her strange talent for "waking dreams," and what triggered it. Knew that the sense had been balky of late.

"Possibly. A feeling of...awe...touched me, as if I was in Jerusalem again." She considered the finger of presence that had beckoned. "There is more to the cave system than the front room. I'll start tonight. Anything from Ling on how they were found?"

"Found or made?"

Brenna smiled at the sharp words. "I think found, if you mean made recently."

Duncan wheezed in reply. "Ling says a shepherd found them–she doesn't know why Strand was called in. She respected the old man's solid technique, but she was no more blind to his limitations than you were."

They were nearly at the top of the mesa. "A people of peace," Brenna murmured in true Gaelic. "How certain can we be that it is still their way?"

"Conquerors come and go, but the Hopi remain. They finally even defeated the mineral exploiters and the Navajo," was Duncan's only answer.

By now Brenna was feeling the effort in her legs. "With the help of the government and the Navajos," was her wry response. "How far would they have gotten if the coal mining had not been destroying the water table? And only the Navajo know why the threat of destroying their ceremonial fetishes caused that land ownership appeal to be dropped." She stopped walking, leaning against the first rocky outcropping of the wall to catch her breath.

"It is a story they keep close to their hearts, how the Hopi came to be the keepers of the Navajo *tiponis*." Duncan had no false pride; he sank against the rock, his breathing slow and deep.

After a sharp glance told her the old man was fine, Brenna looked out over the expanse of earth below, watching it flood with color as the sun rose higher. Sculptured rocks, fleecy sheep, rows of cotton, maize, squash... Heat baked them, light burning into their faces and reminding Brenna she had left her UV block in the camp. Feeling the slow pace steal into her bones, Brenna suddenly thought of her grandmother, and the woman's fierce love of her land. Land Winnifred Carey had died for, as she would have defended her God. Brenna had not been in Wales during the riots; had not been present during either of the incidents that had destroyed both sides of her family.

"Grana would have liked this place," she said aloud, lapsing into true Cymric even as she pushed those thoughts away.

"It's a beautiful region, and the lack of machinery would have pleased her," Duncan said tranquilly.

"No, I mean the living spirit of the lan– "

"What did you say?"

At the soft English question, Brenna nearly jumped off the side of the mesa. She whirled, seeking a source. Only a few rolling pebbles.... Two sleek, dark heads slowly appeared at a hole in the wall, the children studying her thoughtfully.

"Whose words are those?" the older child asked, her English precise.

Brenna smiled faintly. "It is the tongue of my mother's people," Brenna told her in English. "Don't you have a language you use only with your people?"

As the girl nodded solemnly, Brenna continued: "We are the anthropologists who have come to study the cave pictures. I would like to talk to some of your elders, to see if any of them remember stories about the paintings." Bending her knees, Brenna peered through the opening in the wall. "Will you take us to them?"

Another moment, as if of decision, and then: "I'll take you to my *So'o*. Come!" A gesture as swift as her words, and the girl was up and running, vanishing into the pueblos beyond.

"Wait!" What color was her shirt, how tall– Then Brenna realized the younger child remained, shyly watching out of the corner of an eye. Studying the chubby toddler in turn, Brenna decided that it was male. "Will you take Duncan and me into Oraivi?" The youngster nodded, waiting for Duncan to stand. Uncertain, Brenna slowly offered the boy her hand. The child considered the pale, slender fingers, the delicate silver bracelet, and then extended a small, round hand in reply. Looking up at her, he softly said something in Hopi, and then began to lead her into the village.

Brenna could hear chuckling from behind her. "All right, expert– what did he say?"

"The word means 'beautiful,'" Duncan answered in their home-speech, moving up to take her other hand. "I'll leave you to guess if he meant you or the bracelet. The older one is taking us to her grandmother. She used the word for clan mother, so we may get some history after all."

They were surrounded by adobe walls, jutting out of the mesa. If there was a pattern to the town, Brenna couldn't make sense of it; they were lost amid the narrow streets, following a cloud of dust.

The adults walking the streets and working before doorways politely averted their gazes, but Brenna heard the soft flow of Hopi voices behind them, and knew their presence had caused excitement. There had been trouble years ago, with outsiders entering the settlement at will–enough trouble that Oraivi had closed its doors even to scholars. Duncan had not visited the area in almost forty years.

It was a place of contrasts, a land dominated by smell and touch. A warm, capricious wind brought odors to her nose, of bread baking, ground cornmeal, newly-washed wool; the sharp, familiar fragrance of sheep was strangely comforting. In a way, part of her heart had come home. Around Oraivi all things orbited, the spiritual center of the Hopi universe.

They went around another corner and were among a group of children. Solemn, dressed in blue cloth pants and colorful long-sleeved shirts, the young Hopi actually stared at the newcomers in amazement, and were no less awed by the urchin leading them in. Brenna had a sudden fear of an irate Hopi mother rushing up to snatch away her son, but no adults materialized. Duncan sat down on a bench beside the small doorway, and gestured for her to do the same. Before she could join him, the little girl suddenly appeared from the pueblo, seizing her other hand.

"My So'o is asleep, but my brother is coming as soon as his art box finishes spitting up," the girl announced. "What's your name?"

"Ah...Dr. Meghan Stewart," Brenna chose to say. "What's yours?"

This unleashed a flood of answers from the throng, rendering it impossible for her to hear any one name. In the midst of the shouting children and Duncan's amusement, Brenna felt a tug on her sleeve. She had to bend forward to hear the small boy's hesitant English.

"What's your *real* name?"

The question so astonished Brenna she merely stared in response. She did know that the Hopi were like many Amerindians, having both English and private names. But the protocol involved...

Duncan was fighting to control a laugh; he knew how nervous children made her, with their wise eyes and cutting tongues.

Something in the small face, the dark eyes answered her. "Brenna," she murmured to him.

"Renna?" the child attempted.

"B-erenna," the woman emphasized, making the soft "pop" of the consonant.

"There is no 'B' in Hopi," Duncan explained.

"What's it mean?" the boy persisted, as if trying to understand something obscure about her.

Means? Oh, yes– "It means 'raven-haired woman,'" she told the pair holding her hands, hoping her voice did not carry to the noisy group beyond. They were now about five bodies deep in pushing, squirming youngsters.

"Appropriate," said a voice close to her ear. Both children lifted their heads at the word, and the gathering began to quiet down. Looking over her shoulder, Brenna saw a slender man. Dark eyes studied her intently. Lifting her head to meet his gaze, Brenna wondered how long he had been standing there. "Go on," he said finally to the group of children. "They will be here for some time." Duncan helped a tiny girl vacate his lap, and the crowd began to melt away. The Hopi looked pointedly at the children holding Brenna's hands. Sighing, the young girl let go and grabbed for the little one. A few swift words in Hopi, and the child released Brenna.

The woman hesitantly waved good bye, and the two children wiggled fingers back at her before running after their playmates.

"I hope you'll forgive their curiosity," the man said simply. "We have few visitors, and never...a fair, raven-haired woman. They are used to the military ignoring them."

"Of course," Brenna said, not wishing to turn aside any courtesy. Then her humor took hold. "Is your...art box...finished spitting up?"

The man stared blankly at her a moment, and then a smile flashed across his face, revealing startling white teeth against polished copper skin. He pulled a small, square box from his shirt pocket. "Schematics. When the HAL8000 pops the final result– "

"I see," she answered, smiling shyly. "I'm Dr. Meghan Stewart, and this is– "

"One of the few people left who studies individual regions instead of just Amerindians," the man finished for her. "My grandmother cherishes the eight-part vid series you did on Hopi culture. She will be pleased that she lived long enough for you to return. I am David Lansa. Will you come in for cool water or coffee?" With a faint smile, he backed into the adobe home. A moment of hesitation, and Brenna followed him.

The main room was larger than she had expected, its whitewashed ceilings higher. Brenna's eyes rested on the huge stone fireplace, the focal point of the area. Despite the heat a fire was burning brightly, water boiling in a pot. Ladders led up to a higher level; muted sunshine above hinted at solar panels. Other rooms stretched beyond the main living space, the narrow corridors bearing a vague resemblance to the passages below the mesa.

"Please, be seated," David suggested, ushering them to low seats by the cooler, inner wall. He paused by the fireplace mantel, retrieving several mugs, and took out a sealed tin. As he prepared the concoction, Brenna recognized the odor of real coffee. A strange blend of old and new, this man who carried schematics in his worn shirt pocket. A shagged, feathered haircut in the latest style, and faded indigo pants of a material she had not seen in years. Cotton was something you found scraps of in South American graves...rubbing her hand down the smooth, semi-permeable fabric of her skin-tight, flaming red pants, she kept her thoughts to herself.

Finally Lansa handed them mugs of steaming coffee and then folded cross-legged to the woven floor mats. "What name do you prefer, doctors?" He eyed Brenna steadily.

"Duncan will suffice for me, as always, but my niece will have to speak for herself." He glanced briefly at Brenna as he spoke.

She understood his meaning. She never introduced herself as Brenna; it was a nickname Grana had given her as a child, and had been kept within the family. Something in the little boy had called it from her.

"My parents named me Meghan," she started slowly. "Somehow I have never felt tough enough to be 'the strong one.' What name do you prefer?"

"I?" Lansa studied her for a long moment. "Kúivato. But David Lansa is simpler. Lansa means the spear or lance, and since the 90s my family has been the thrown weapon of the Hopi. We are almost a splinter clan unto ourselves, though we have no rites in the yearly cycle. We go out and abroad, paving the way to modern society, choosing the best of the new world to bring back to our people." After a moment, he added: "I don't know what 'David' means."

"Are you of your grandmother's clan, David?" Duncan asked, sipping at his coffee.

"Parrot," the man confirmed. Duncan nodded thoughtfully.

"The reason we have come, Mr. Lansa, is to ask if your elders can tell us anything about the pictures in the caves," Brenna started, balancing the mug of strong brew on the edge of her seat.

"Caves? I thought...there was just the one."

"There is something beyond the front grotto; we haven't examined it, yet."

David did not change expression. "Silena mentioned only the one room. He was the man who found it—he had lost a sheep, and thought a coyote might have dragged off the remains." The man paused to drink some coffee. "May I ask if you've spoken to Asbin yet?"

"Briefly," Brenna said, her mind's eye returning momentarily to the shadowed televid image of a man as neutral as his cinder block building—silver hair, gray NorAmerican Forces uniform, eyes the color of old snow.

Lansa's eyes seemed to smile grimly. "He told you little of the incidents here?"

"We know that two accidents have taken place," Brenna told him, her gaze never leaving his face. "And that Strand's work has been removed by estate authorities." This last grated; the legal intricacies were so involved Strand's results would be duplicated before the originals were released. After consideration, she added: "Asbin suspects the paintings and carvings are fakes, to hold up construction of the control site." It was a struggle to control a cynical smile; "control site" was such an innocent name for what was essentially a cluster of anti-terrorist launching silos.

Duncan leaned back against the wall, settling in. David's face was expressionless. One slender finger traced the rim of his mug; the pause was a long one.

"I sent for Dr. Strand," the Hopi said finally. "Not because of his reputation, but because I knew he had just finished a semester and could arrive immediately. I feared the military might tamper with the paintings. I know what *I* think they are–at least the first chamber, I have not been deeper into the cave–but what matters is what you tell the military they are. The NorAmerican Forces intend to gut that cave for their control room."

When the silence had gone on too long, Brenna asked: "Has Asbin confronted your elders with his theory that Navajos or Hopis killed Dr. Strand?"

Lansa's eyes hardened like basalt. "They questioned villagers for days. Desperation can drive people to horrible deeds, but no Navajo or Hopi killed Dr. Strand. Why would we? He was on the verge of proving that the paintings were of Hopi origin, guaranteeing their safety." His voice softened. "But this would be the best site, and the political stability of both hemispheres deteriorates. I often wonder what Asbin's orders truly are."

Despite the growing heat, his words chilled Brenna. And she had been naive enough to think that she'd left nuclear threats behind when she left Europe. War escalating among a myriad of ancient enemies scattered throughout Asia, Africa, Europe– *When will we learn we are Human first, and that all other names are merely changes of clothing?* She knew she had not kept up with international news, the past year or so, but information had only depressed her.

A woman stepped into the room, breaking off Brenna's thoughts. Nodding politely to their guests, she spoke swiftly to David in Hopi. The young man acknowledged her words by setting down his mug. "My great-grandmother is awake," he said softly. "I don't think she can help you, but she will see you now." With that, he rose to his feet, leading the way into the inner sanctuary of the house to a tiny, wizened woman whose memories spanned a thousand years.

Ten thousand years, Brenna thought. That, David had said, was how long people had lived on the mesas. The image held her silent as she followed Duncan carefully down the dark footpath, her eyes following the beam of the HyLites provided by the Hopi. An hour had stretched into meals and a day. David had been correct–the pictographs, even the caves, had been beyond the collective memory of the Hopi elders who came to speak. But Brenna had sat enthralled by their stories, as they related their tales of the last hundred years and of legends older than themselves.

One clan history in particular intrigued her. All the clans had special ceremonies that demonstrated their powers, gifts from the Creator Taiowa to aid rainfall, fertility, planting, and healing. These ceremonies determined each clan's place in the pecking order of Hopi life, an order that began with the ruling Bear Clan and continued on down. All except the Coyote Clan. They were as they had been from the very beginning; the guardian clan. The ones to scout ahead the paths of their people's journeys to be sure they were safe; the ones who brought up the rear of every ceremonial procession, guarding against evil. Coyote Clan was named in the ancient prophecies–the last to leave any legendary village along the path of the Hopi migration to Oraivi; the ones who would "close the door" upon this world, the Hopi's mythological fourth world. The ones to herald the end of all things.

"Where will they be if the legends die?" she murmured, and then caught herself up. Another saying of her grandmother's. Severed from her past, Brenna felt an elusive kinship with the Hopi, as they struggled to retain their beliefs in a world leeched of faith. To face every ghost, to learn from past lives, understand what those people were and meant to be...even as her own presence stirred latent images quiescent in the very air around her. Images engraved in the memories of the stones themselves.

Shivering in the cooling desert air, Brenna shoved the thoughts back into the depths of her mind. It was gone, all of it–no sense in raking through her own pain. It was but a grain of sand in the weathering of the world.

"Let's go to the caves," Duncan said suddenly. "The waxing moon beckons. Perhaps we should have taken David up on his offer of Coyote guards on the site."

"Were you planning on explaining it to Asbin, or were you going to leave it to me?" she murmured, considering her possible level of authority. Asbin had sent a soldier up earlier, to ask when she was returning to the camp. To ask, not to demand–not the usual military tone of voice. David's farewell threaded the river of her thoughts.

Kúivato, she had called him, and he had shown no surprise at her memory. *It means 'Greeting the Sun;' David is simpler*, had been his response. *But you did not give me a name. Brenna*, she had told him, because it felt right–

"I think they're grooming David to be chief. The elders obviously think quite a bit of him," Duncan went on as they neared the end of the trail.

"I thought chiefs must be of the Bear Clan," Brenna said, forcing herself to concentrate on his words.

"Bear Clan is dying out. The rulers of the next world will be Parrot Clan. David seems intelligent and farsighted; I think he'd make a good chief." Duncan paused before the entrance to the cave, flicking the HyLite to bright beam. The young soldiers on guard duty shifted nervously in the light. "Go on in, Brenna. I want to talk to them."

Brenna did not argue. Military guards, no matter how distressed, held no interest for her. Illuminaries blazed as she entered the passageway. She paused, watching the play of light and shadow flash across the rock walls. Vivid drawings leapt out at her, mellowed by the indirect radiance.

Old, extremely old...Brenna could feel the weight of eons in their lines. A-Ttavitt's readings were on filatape, carefully tacked beneath each image; Asbin was selective about what he would force them to repeat. Tomorrow Brenna would bring her black box in and start on the corridor paintings—thank the powers that be for the paintings, petroglyphs were harder to date—

"Blessings, child, here's an interesting sight," Duncan murmured as he came up behind her. "What's all the fuss about? These are plainly Hopi symbols. See, here is the *nakwách* of brotherhood," he began, pointing to the curious carving that was reminiscent of the Chinese yin-yang symbol. "Brenna, this is—this is the Creation Myth! I've never heard of it being on a cave wall. No wonder Strand was so excited. Damn it, what a time for this to turn up."

"What do you mean?" she asked softly in home-speech.

He did not look at her, his gaze on a carving. "There's a warhead in orbit."

The silence in the cave was absolute. Brenna directed her borrowed HyLite toward the ceiling, looking for more carvings or paintings. Ancient campfires had burned within this place...the carbon build-up needed to be measured— She considered asking who had launched the device, but thought better of it. Did it really matter what terrorist or nationalist group was flexing its muscles this week? Eventually one of them would launch a makeshift device, a faulty control box activating the head or damaging the targeting mechanism, and then...

"They can't declare an emergency overriding historical Class One statutes without a seven-day grace period," Duncan murmured, stepping farther into the cave. "There should be time to image them, date them...leave something for the future."

"Future?" The bitterness churning just beneath the surface welled up in her. Fragments of the past, obliterated in the name of age-old hatreds, divisions— "If we destroy the past, can we have a future without repeating every mistake we've ever made? What happens when we've killed all the legends? Grana always threw that in my face, when I told her religion was dead. What is left, now that reason, too, has failed us?"

"Not our question, lass. Clear your mind and reach out. I'm going to try and see into that second chamber." Without pause Duncan started patting his clothes, looking for his borrowed HyLite.

Wordlessly Brenna extended her light to him, touching his cheek in thanks for the anchor he had provided to her life. Piece-meal wars, ravaging the roots of humanity– Sighing, she tried to push it aside, opening her mind to whatever power lingered in the cave. All she could do was relax; the energy chose whether or not to acknowledge her presence.

Once again a feeling of unease. That gentle feeling of incredible strength, unfathomable depth–she drew back, pulling into her own consciousness. Usually it was visual images, tri-dee color imprints of the past, of the individuals who had painted and carved their records. This sensation had been present before, but never dominant, never overwhelming everything else. It reminded her too much of the state of meditation...prayer...of all she had lost when the Highlands burned, the land and all her father's family save Duncan. The sensation had vanished, then...*or did you cease to open yourself to it?*

She heard Duncan rattling around in the back, sliding pebbles, his grumbling–a sharply caught breath.

"Brenna! Good Lord, Brenna, come and *look!*"

Leaping to her feet, Brenna moved into the passage. Duncan's legs were visible ahead, still protruding from the opening into the other chamber. Abruptly the light dimmed–a large beam had burnt out, only the illuminary by the outer door remaining. Brenna was plunged into murk, her reference point a needle slice of Duncan's reflected light.

"Ah, Duncan," she began quietly, uncertain where to put her feet. In response the man activated the back button of his tiny light, flashing it briefly at her knees, and–

The ceiling broke loose, chunks of rock hailing down before her, dust rising in choking clouds, obliterating light and sound and–

Brenna spent the following day in the ancient cubicle. She accepted Duncan's death stoically, a selfish corner of her heart thinking it was inevitable–she had lost everyone else, why not Duncan? How ironic to finally meet Asbin over her uncle's body. Ignoring her cuts and bruises, she remained on the cot, clutching a piece of the rock that had fallen on them. It was a stalemate; she could scarcely think, but she would not leave.

And she had nightmares. Tons of rock, falling on her, annihilating the heritage of her people, destroying the remnants of Keltic history. A man with Asbin's face chipping away at hieroglyphics, petroglyphs, erasing the past. Her grandmother's voice, arguing, scolding, warning her of people with agendas, how could she have been so foolish, scientists were always expendable– *Pe cymmerwn adenydd y wawr, a phe trigwn yn eithafoedd y môr: Yno hefyd y'm tywysai dy law, ac y'm daliai dy ddeheulaw.*

She woke with the words of the psalm on her lips, sitting bolt upright on the cot.

"Brenna, can you hear me?" David knelt beside her, shaking her gently.

"How long?" she whispered.

"This is the second morning. You were...chanting...in your sleep, in another tongue," he said quietly.

"Home-speech," was her terse reply as the dream flooded back to her. "From psalms. It's about–it's about running from God. 'If I take the wings of morning, and dwell in the uttermost parts of the sea, even there shall thy hand lead me, and thy right hand hold me.' David, I dreamt that the legends died."

"Have they?" After a moment he set his hand lightly over hers. "I'm sorry. He was a fine man."

There was a long moment of silence, and then Brenna asked conversationally: "Perhaps the legends have not yet died. Where is Asbin?"

"Squatting in the blockhouse like a spider. There are six guards left; two on Asbin's quarters, four guarding the troop carrier and A-Ttavitt cataloging fragments, as you instructed." At her blank look, he said gently: "The last order you gave your assistant. All nations with missile capability have been put on alert, the Americas included. Only a half-dozen soldiers can be spared for rocks."

"Then I might as well continue working," Brenna whispered, exhaustion creeping through her bones.

"Asbin wants you to continue."

"Why?"

It was more rhetorical than anything else, but David said: "I think he hopes this is another false alarm, and that he will have time to entrench."

She heard the judgment in his voice. "But– "

David shrugged. "I think his superiors have abandoned him. And I am grateful we are in the middle of nowhere...the center of my universe."

Standing, Brenna moved past him, pausing in the door frame to greet the sunrise. No joy in it– "Please follow me." She walked briskly toward the cave opening.

One of the soldiers appeared as she neared the entrance. His young face was devoid of emotion. *Had he caused Duncan's death?* Paranoia was being passed like a virus....

"Doctor, no outsiders are allowed to enter the cave unless– "

"Mr. Lansa is an engineer. He is going to check the structural support, to try and anticipate landslides," Brenna announced, climbing the entry rubble. She stopped moving at the sight of three newcomers walking up the shattered rock behind her. Two of the Hopi were young men, perhaps David's age. The third was much older, graying yet still hale, with the ageless eyes of all Hopi elders.

"This is Pamösi, Paul Fog, the leader of the Coyote Clan, and two *Qaletaqa*–Guardians. They have offered to watch outside the caves," David explained.

"For what?" the soldier asked, his reserve ruffled.

"Evil spirits?" Brenna suggested, and then propelled herself past him into the cave.

The passage was broader than she remembered; higher. The aging illuminaries blazed on–the soldiers had patched the defective one back together, Brenna noted. The passage to the second chamber had been cleared of rock and reinforced, Duncan's body undoubtedly sealed in a bag and awaiting transport. The soldiers had created a ramp to reach the second chamber.

What was Asbin thinking of? What was he doing, supervising this crumbling site? *What am I doing here?*

"I am an ecological engineer, Brenna. But I will help you as I can," David said, coming up behind her. He had brought another HyLite, and was carefully examining the wall and ceiling porta-struts in the brilliance of its white light.

Brenna reached for the only disconnected illuminary, wrestling it onto the ramp. She would see the second chamber–all of it–without any more delay. "Why did our pilot tell us your people are expecting rain?" she asked between shoves.

"Let me help. Because it is the time of the Snake-Antelope Ceremony, to bring rain for the final maturity of the crops. It is almost complete; I will arrange for you to see the Snake Dance on the last day." David pushed the illuminary to the top of the ramp, switched it on, and shoved it ahead of himself into the grotto.

Brenna half-expected to see the carvings defaced, but the dream had not been literal. There were no fresh scars–all was as Duncan must have seen it. She climbed over the illuminary, wondering if she had totally misunderstood Asbin; if he neither helped nor hindered because it did not matter, it had never mattered, it was all illusion...all mere appearances. In the end they would be destroyed.

Petroglyphs–an entire wall of them. Brenna sat upon a ledge, carefully leaning back, her eyes taking in the details. From the passage came a sound of exclamation. Flicking a glance to one side, she realized that surprise, not injury, had prompted the gasp–David was also staring at the wall. After watching him sink down upon the ramp of rubble, Brenna turned back to the carvings.

It was an unusual grouping; divided into four areas, each area divided again, making a total of eight sections. One set of carvings had a line jutting across a corner, as if to symbolize a break. Brenna considered the designs...human figures, bear tracks, snakes, cornstalks, nakwách brotherhood symbols. Stone dust lay in piles beneath the mural, undisturbed for centuries.

One chip of stone was different–darker. Standing, Brenna moved to the wall and picked it up. Portions of carvings were on either side. "I wonder what this is from," she said aloud. "David, you must be my Hopi source." Somehow she couldn't trust A-Ttavitt now. "I know these carvings only in relation to world petroglyphs. I can determine their age, but without something concrete leading to a known people, I can't begin to prove their source is Proto-Hopi."

"How do you normally determine source?" David asked, taking the fragment from her. His face stilled as he looked at it.

Brenna considered the question, and then grinned without mirth. Why not? Who would believe him, if she chose to deny it? "The energy left in the carvings...reanimates...and shows me the circumstances under which the image was created," she said swiftly, embarrassed to hear the words spoken aloud. Only Duncan had known for certain of her talent, although Brenna believed Grana had suspected.

David did not smile. "You mean the spirits reveal themselves to you?" he asked.

"Who said anything about spirits?" she retorted, moving to the petroglyphs. "Are any of the carvings familiar?"

"I think I know exactly what they are. The Hopi have four sacred tablets, stones of prophecy we have held in our hearts for centuries. These carvings match the ones on the tablets."

Brenna swiftly turned. "Exactly? Your tablets are copies of this wall?"

"Or the walls are copies. Our legends say we entered this world at the spiritual center of the universe, but we had to make our migrations to the four corners of the continent to weed out all the latent evil of the previous world." This was half to himself. Brenna felt a chill as she watched David examine the dark rock fragment. "Oraivi is the site we finally returned to, all clans, dependent on our mighty Creator for rainfall and life. To think that our Emergence and Ending might be the same place." He looked up, smiling, as if to reassure her he had not lost his mind. "Never laugh at a legend. It may come back to haunt you. May I borrow this? I'd like to take it to the leader of the Fire clan. We may be able to help you after all. And you, us."

Brenna nodded, mystified, as David stood to leave. "Interpret your dream, Brenna. I think it will answer almost everything." And he left.

The dream? First engineer, then mystic, and now psychologist–

"Dr. Stewart?" The light from the first chamber was blocked by several shadowy figures. It was the elusive Asbin, looking pinched, a living skull with haunted eyes. Ling A-Ttavitt was among the group amassed at his back.

"Colonel," she said neutrally.

"We must prepare to evacuate; our orders are to leave at 0600 tomorrow. The defense effort has reached Crisis One proportions, and– "

"Where could be safer than a million miles from anywhere?" Brenna asked conversationally.

Asbin blinked, and then seemed to regroup his thoughts. "Surely you wish to be with your family at– "

"My family," she interrupted him, "died in this cave. If the world is changing irrevocably, let me try to save a piece of the past." Her gaze flicked beyond him to the shade that was A-Ttavitt. "Bring me the black box. Put it in the first chamber, and start imaging the pictographs." To Asbin she said: "I am making progress, and prefer to remain here." The look she gave the officer was direct as she gestured at the petroglyphs. "I'm a Kelt, colonel, and Kelts aren't afraid to die."

Asbin considered her a moment, and then pivoted toward his following. "Get the imager," he told the motionless A-Ttavitt.

Only then did the site artist start out the stone corridor.

Brenna left Ling A-Ttavitt working in the first chamber and strolled into the second, the black box swinging from one hand. At least the girl was willing to work one more day. David Lansa was taking a long time...she became conscious of hunger, of how long it had been since she had eaten. Dust sifted down into her hair. *Interpret your dream.* No, thank you. Her dreams were often frightening. Better to work on the walls. Carefully she positioned the instrument, sampling one of the incised lines, seeking trace elements from carving tools, exposure rates, organic materials. The light sequence flashed as the box began compiling information. Why had she taken this accursed job? To please her uncle. Where was David? Who could interpret these, now that Duncan–

She felt a pang at his name, the first real mote of grief she had allowed herself. And the delicate chill slid around her, encouraging her thought–*encouraging*? Shaking, Brenna set the black box down on the dirt floor. It hummed along, oblivious to her discomfort. But something was aware of her thoughts, her feelings. Or someone. A question rose from her subconscious. Vainly she tried to suppress it. What if...what if what she had felt all these years was not pure energy, but cognizant spirit? What if... Brenna sat down in the soft soil, ignoring the waves of dust rising into the stale air. Soundlessly she felt the pieces of her dream fit themselves into a giant picture. The Keltic heritage destroyed, ripped apart by the Eurasian Forces. Her guilt at not being with her family...of living when they had died. Her fierce crusade to protect the relics of other pasts, other peoples. And her strange link to Grana, to the old woman's belief.

The scientist bowed her head to her knees, unsure whether she was a fraud or one of the privileged few able to tap into the universal consciousness. What it was, why it spoke to her– Whispering aloud, she addressed it in a language she understood: "I have done nothing of myself. I am but a vessel to be filled with what must be remembered."

Amazingly, there was no bitterness in the thought, only wonder. Later to think it through, to wrestle with this intelligence, to demand explanation and understanding of those wars, deaths, pain. Now there was only the moment; she had a source to explain the petroglyphs to her. Only a slip of thought, in the home-speech: *I will not fight you anymore.*

Presence grew within her, welling up like water so pure she was certain she would never thirst again. With it came understanding. Staring at the petroglyphs, Brenna knew their meaning, tried to verbalize their prophecy. It was like the echo of a voice whispering from the past....

After the clans reach their final home, the time will come when they will be conquered by a strange people. They will be forced to pattern their land and lives after these strangers, or be punished horribly. But they are not to resist, for a deliverer will come. Their lost white brother, Pahána, will bring them the missing corner of the Fire Clan tablet, deliver them from their conquerors, and point the way toward a universal brotherhood of mankind. But until that coming, to leave the Hopi way will bring evil upon the tribes, and the Bear Clan leader will then have to be beheaded to dispel the evil.

The land between the two rivers is yours. Other tales... Brenna suddenly came back from the shadows, the ancient, quivering voice of a clan leader fading into the silence. She had *seen* the fire, the fire that had blackened the ceiling above her, the great man giving the tablets to the clan leaders, the making of prayer sticks and the chanting. The youths carving the story on the walls, copying the tablets. Tears had crept down her cheeks sometime during her trance; idly she brushed at the dusty tracks with the back of one hand. *Ah, Duncan, I will save this cave for you...I will remember it.*

Preoccupied, Brenna rose to her feet, touching the black box in passing. With any luck there would be enough evidence from the lab tests to narrow the dates, confirm her vision, give the Hopi back their sacred chamber–

Slanting sunlight drew her out of her thoughts. It was getting late; she would have to– And then Brenna was outside, and she forgot what she was going to do. The two Coyote Clan *Qaletaqa* still stood guard, but Pamösi, their leader, was waiting at the foot of the path. He gestured for Brenna to follow him.

Momentarily she held her ground. Other visions had told her that the people of peace had shed blood in the past, when they felt their way of life was threatened. Then she moved to the clan leader's side.

Old Pamösi did not speak as they walked up the trail, his gait the equal of any man in his prime. Several times he stopped to let Brenna rest, but he offered no information, not even to explain David's absence. When they neared the top, Pamösi let her walk ahead of him, moderating his pace.

A silent crowd was waiting for them. Brenna slowed, confused, when she realized that four lines of cornmeal had been drawn across the trail. Pamösi had halted also; he waited quietly behind her. Searching the weathered faces of the gathering, Brenna realized that the village elders made up the majority of those present. She recognized David standing on the fringe of the group, his warm eyes reassuring. The elderly Bear Clan leader stood in the front; last of his line, spokesman of his people. Bright eyes peered at her from a wrinkled face; the man's withered hand did not shake as he extended it, palm up, to the young woman.

Brenna fought to control her trembling. David had the carved rock fragment–what else did the leader expect? She stood motionless while the sun went down into a sea of sharp flame and the air grew cold. Even the cave spirit held back, waiting.

Tragedy in their past, but in the beginning they were a people of peace. With no other guidance, Brenna followed her heart, extending her hand palm-down to clasp the aged leader's hand.

A murmuring grew, like the roar of a seashell in her ears. The old man still held her hand, and Brenna could see his eyes were filled with tears. David was suddenly beside them.

"I–don't understand," she started softly.

David's answer was laughter ringed in warmth. "You think too much, Brenna! You hold in your hand the nakwách. You are Pahána, bringing universal brotherhood to the people of peace."

"I am the Pahána? David– " her voice dropped to a hiss. "The Pahána is a white *man*– "

"Oh, I know," he said, his smile contagious. "The clan leaders had trouble with that, too. But you have fulfilled their prophecies, Brenna. They cannot deny you!"

In the midst of the crowd's excitement, a man behind them cried out something in Hopi, and all voices were extinguished, snuffed out like a torch. Brenna and David turned to face Pamösi and the breathless young man beside him. The youth continued speaking, his face strained and his words trembling.

David grew very still. "The warhead has dropped from orbit. It landed in India." Turning to the Bear Clan leader, he whispered something, even as Brenna looked away from the gathering, unwilling to face the Hopi as mass destruction mocked the advent of their universal brotherhood.

"Asbin's receiver is stronger than ours," David said softly. "Let us see what he has picked up on satellite."

The clan leaders began to descend to the desert floor.

It was hard for Brenna in the darkness, doubly bitter when she saw the air car lift off. It was Pamösi who picked her up when she faltered, carrying her like a small child.

Silence reigned on the flats, broken only by the shout of the young Coyote guard who still waited by the empty cave. The camp had been stripped; only the foam cubes and Asbin's headquarters remained. At first they thought Brenna alone had been left behind, until they approached the cinder block building. They could hear weeping within. Pamösi set Brenna back on her feet, but walking toward the door did not trigger the sensors.

The electronic eye was broken. Brenna knew there had to be an emergency switch. She tripped the lock with a swing of her arm; the panel responded, sliding open. Static and garbled voices struck them like a gust of wind. Ling huddled near the doorway, sobbing hysterically, oblivious to their arrival. Asbin's seated profile was just visible in the gloom beyond. David started toward the man, speaking his name. It seemed unreal to Brenna, who focused on Ling, pulling her to one side while a village elder stepped over them and adjusted the delicate tuning of the receiver.

"He's dead," came a voice. Brenna looked up, and wished that she had not. Despite the growing darkness, she could see a dark spot on Asbin's forehead. Self-inflicted? Was this the cause of Ling's frenzy? The result? Because of the warhead, or their abandonment, or... Brenna held the tiny woman close, willing herself not to think.

Everyone seated themselves on the floor, listening to the babble of languages coming in over the airwaves. The Bear Clan leader flipped the dial at will, seeking the strongest signals. Some of the voices were calm, islands of tranquillity in the face of disaster. Others were edging hysteria, as reports continued to flow in. It had not stopped with the terrorist groups' orbiting warhead. For the first time, Brenna truly understood the definition of the word "escalation."

She listened with little comprehension, drawing meaning from inflection as the night wore on. Myriad stars appeared in the night sky, a glittering wall of obsidian beyond the open door. David sat down next to her, although she did not remember him leaving Asbin. No one stirred; their entire existence was bound up in sound.

"'Beloved,'" Brenna said at one point, and David shifted beside her. "Your name means 'beloved.'" He did not speak.

At last the broadcasts began to thin. Brenna first noticed the absence of the squeaky-voiced announcer. Signing off, their transmissions cut off? One strong signal vanished literally between one word and the next, and Brenna wondered if a satellite had been destroyed. How long to get another back up there.... Other signals faded–losing power, afraid to provide a target, allowing EBS to kick in?

And then the Bear Clan leader flipped the communicator switch, silencing the gibbering machine. Stillness wrapped itself around the group, weaving among them like a physical force. Even Ling had ceased to weep.

Momentarily, Brenna thought of protesting the man's action; only a moment. Then she noticed the silence...the presence beyond the waiting. And she began to wonder if the Hopi, like herself, could hear stone speak.

The group waited awhile, but the night offered no other messages; finally the clan leaders began exiting the blockhouse, supporting the steps of the eldest among them. Brenna waited until most of them had left before she helped Ling stand. Sighing, she turned to David, trying to think of something to say, but gentle fingers to her lips stopped her. Only Pamösi waited with them.

David reached over and took Ling's arm. Together they helped the woman out the doorway. Behind them, Pamösi raised his arm, closing the door.

The flames rose higher, licking, curling at the ceiling–collapsing on themselves as Brenna came back to herself. A gust of cold wind rounded the corner, tickling her feet. With a sigh she shook back her silver hair, smoothing the warm wool dress over her exposed, wrinkled hands. This time she had seen the Coyote-Swallow race at Sikyatki, the legendary home of the migrating Coyote Clan. She glanced at the entranceway; the light was dim. It was late, and she was tired....

"Grana!" The clear voice echoed against the chamber walls, and the fire leapt in response.

Smiling, Brenna shouted: "Who are you? Come in!"

A hesitant youth slid into the outer corridor, barely discernible behind the flames. "It is Chöviohóya, Grana. Chief-father has prepared our dinner, and asks that you bid the spirits farewell for a time." The boy began to back out.

"Young Deer!" she said softly in the home tongue, and he paused; he was one of the few who had learned it, and would deny her nothing when she spoke it. "Don't you like my cave?"

"Of course, Grana."

"Then why do you leave so swiftly? Do you fear it?"

"I fear nothing!" he said adamantly, taking one step back inside.

"Not even the sky falling? Even the bravest warriors of all feared the wrath of the gods. I think it is not the cave that you fear, but what is inside yourself." Silence. "I can help you face it." More silence, but the child did not retreat. "You can learn much from listening to the Great Spirit, and always return to walk in the light of day." Slowly the boy slipped into the first chamber, studying his grandmother with no small amount of awe. He had David's face, but her own father's broad shoulders and long legs. Shooting up like the corn.... "Sit by me."

David would be wondering about them. But, after a bit, he would understand, and rejoice.

"What can you teach me, Grana?" the youth asked, his voice hushed.

"What would you know first? You are born of three great heritages, Chöviohóya. What would you know?"

"Will you tell me of the beginning, when the guardian spirit Másaw gave the sacred tablets to our people? And about the white warriors, who feared nothing but the sky falling?"

"That part is past, child," she said gently, "for I have seen the sky fall, and I do not fear it anymore." Brenna cleared her throat. *"After the clans reached their final home—"*

Intro for Ducks

Once upon a time at the World Fantasy Convention, I was part of a group lunching with writer Jane Yolen. She had decided to do YA anthologies with Martin Greenberg, about werewolves, vampires, and so on. We were discussing what kind of tales would fit into the package she was assembling, since knowing Jane, it could not be just any werewolf or vampire.

At one point, I asked, "Does the werewolf have to be seen?" Jane's response was, "The werewolf does not have to be seen, but its presence has to be felt."

Her words brought two brief, intense images to mind. One was of a girl walking a path through a farm yard, her shawl pulled tightly around her against the cold, pausing by the side of a wooden building to see withered garlic plants struggling to push their way up through the dirt. Glancing up, she saw the plants were beneath a window. The second vision was that same young woman, dressed simply in a long skirt and shirt, her long blonde braids hanging down, climbing onto a chair and hanging a braid of garlic over an interior door.

That was it. Alfreda Golden-Tongue was born in that moment. She was so intense, I had to check around to make sure I wasn't creating a pale imitation of someone else's character. But no—Allie was her own person, and she had her own story to tell. In Jane Yolen's anthology, Alfreda lived in a post-apocalyptic world, because she had to live someplace where werewolves might be real. But in the novels *Night Calls* and *Kindred Rites*, Allie lived in an alternative history, familiar and yet different from our own.

In *Night Calls* Allie began training to be a practitioner, a person who dealt with werewolves and vampires, who knew magic and herb lore and how to exorcise a ghost. In *Kindred Rites*, Allie began to learn midwifery and ritual spells. She also was kidnapped, and in a bid for freedom began lessons with Death himself, learning how to control Wild Magic, the magic found beyond ritual.

Alfreda also needed to know how to take care of herself in the woods, since she was a frontier dweller. In chapter ten of *Night Calls*, Allie referred to learning how to "duck blind." But she chose not to tell that tale, not at that moment.

In "Ducks," Allie does not learn rituals or spells or even herb lore—she learns how to hunt ducks without a weapon. She also learns the price of that skill, and that everything is answered in time...if you're paying attention.

Ducks

A rising run of notes echoed through the woods, trilling like a flute, and I paused, still bent over a tussock of reeds.

I knew that bird...it had haunted me from the first moment I had heard its song. Sometimes in dreams I saw myself standing outside in the gloom, my shawl pulled tight around my shoulders, the withered shoots of garlic at my feet...the echo of music quavering from the woods beyond.

I could not hide from that bird! Why had it sung in winter? Why was it still singing in the month of Sun, long after most eggs had hatched and babies were fledging? How could I be so sure it was the same bird, when I was miles away from where we had run our trap line?

Was it a bird? I was not so sure....

"Hurry up, Allie," my brother Josh said impatiently as he took my handful of rushes. "We need to get into the water. Papa expects us to get a duck today."

As if I needed the reminder. One last glance over my shoulder, and I turned back to the water's edge. There were four of us in this classroom of sorts—myself, my older brother Joshua, and our neighbors Shaw Kristinsson and Wylie Adamsson-but these classes were for me. I was the one with the second sight...I was the one who heard werewolves keening and dreamt true dreams.

A practitioner needed not only magic and medicine; a practitioner needed herbs and wood lore. But tracking and hunting were useful for any man, living as far west as Ohio and the Northwest Territory beyond. With my oldest brother Dolph dead and only the little boys following us, Josh was needed on the trap line come winter.

I'd be needed, too, someday, but probably not for trapping. I'd lost one brother to the dark on the other side, nipped by a werewolf. Death would have to arm-wrestle me for anyone else.

"Al-lee! Stop woolgathering!" Josh yelled.

Looking back, I could see that Wylie and Shaw were about finished tying on their collars of dusty green leaves. They were blending in nicely with the rim of the little lake–at least from the neck up.

You see, the idea was to look like a floating tussock. The reeds towered over Wylie and Shaw's heads, making them look like they were standing in a field of grass. This trap was easiest for Shaw, with his dark mane–if we ever had to depend on this trick for dinner, the rest of us would need to dirty or dye our hair. Right now we relied on thick leaves and stems.

I used my new knife to cut Josh a few more rushes, and then chose a clump for my own disguise. Cutting vegetation let me forget that the practice was over...today Papa expected us to really grab a duck. And since I was pretty good at pretending to be marsh grass, I had no excuse to miss.

Lord, I didn't want to drown a duck. I knew this was silly–I'd spent the winter and spring learning how to set traps that worked, and I'd scraped more pelts than I could easily count–but there was something about grabbing duck feet and yanking down....

It didn't take long to have more grass than I could use, plus some cattails and a few of those sectioned tubes we've always called snake sticks. I carefully wiped clean my knife on the indigo tail of my cotton shirt and tucked it into its sheath. Then I started twisting and peeling reeds to make strands long enough to tie around my neck. I could cheat, of course, and tuck them into the collar of my shirt, but what if someday I needed to try this without clothes?

Not if Momma had anything to say about it. She was mad enough about Papa teaching me to swim, much less the lessons with Josh, Wylie and Shaw. She put her foot down firmly on the idea of us in the water stark naked. Granted, I don't look much like a woman, yet, but I suppose it wouldn't have been a good idea. So the boys wore old worn pants, and I wore a sleeveless tunic with a skirt that reached to my knees. I think Momma thought I was wearing leggings under it, but I got by with my linings. Who needed the weight on legs and feet? I mean, legs are legs.

Although the sun was still under the rim of the world, I wasn't cold at all. In some ways the month of Sun was my favorite, because there's all that wonderful heat, but none of the stickiness of the month of Fruit. I couldn't see far in the dusty light, but the sound of soft ripples pushing against the shore meant that Shaw and Wylie were already in the water.

Once I had my disguise adjusted to my satisfaction, I set my knife over on a tree stump where the boys had piled their things. Papa was somewhere nearby, but he never hovered–he just told us what to do and then disappeared. That morning he'd said: "I want you four to duck blind today, and catch Sunday dinner." In other words, be floating bushes.

'Course, the boys just had to catch–and maybe pluck–a duck. I'd have to cook and season it, too. Sometimes I thought God must be female, because life had entirely too many little things that were needful, and women were best at handling the little things.

I didn't want to drown a duck. Sure, Cousin Cory had said the ducks had a fighting chance, and I knew what he meant–if the duck wasn't fooled by my clump of weeds, then the duck wouldn't come close. And if the duck was stronger than I was, it didn't matter if the duck was fooled–it could pull away and take off. But I–well, you know my feelings on the subject.

Why didn't I want to grab a duck? Good question. I didn't have an answer, not at that point, but I'd been right glad that all those trap line animals had done their dying when I wasn't around.

Wylie and Josh looked solemn, like they were going into church or something. I'd never thought of a bush as looking serious–it was almost worth a giggle. They made fairly good bushes, if a bit rigid. Both of them splashed too much when they swam, so I expected them to sneak around the lip of the lake and settle over where the water lilies grew.

Shaw and I were better swimmers, so we had the entire shallow cove to choose from. I slipped off my shoes and tossed them by the clothes. My toes were begging for some sand to twitch in, and this lovely waterway was mostly sand at our end.

It was light enough that I could see Josh creeping into the water lilies. A couple of angry quacks made me look up, but there was no thrashing going on anywhere. Wylie's voice floated across the cove.

"Watch out for that lil' point–there's a Momma mallard there with a mess of ducklings, and she's in a pecking mood. Those babies aren't worth the catching, anyway. They're no more than a bite of fluff."

Wish he hadn't said that. Lord, I never want to be hungry enough to eat baby ducks.

"Baby ducks ain't Sunday dinner," Josh whispered loudly.

Good thinking, Joshua. I paused a moment at land's end, letting cool water lap my toes, and then I started in. The weeds were few this close to shore, but I moved very slowly, more to keep from getting tangled than for noise. Sounds don't count until you're eye level with ducks...then they might figure out you're not what you seem. Tall humans they avoided, but sneaky little shrubs?

The cove was shallow enough to have cooled off some during the night, but it wasn't bad if you kept moving. Float with the waves, move with the wind. Drift with the waves...I let my arms move out away from me, still below the surface but near shoulder height. All I had to do was keep my weedy face above water.

I found a good spot near a few other tussocks. It was still pretty sandy, but with more weeds anchored around. I was able to touch bottom and even bend my knees, which meant good traction if I needed it. Now there was nothing left to do but watch and wait.

If I was gonna drown a duck, I was gonna get it right the first time. That duck was never going to know what hit it.

Dawn had finally arrived, glittering off water shining like polished metal. Things are sharp at the moment of sunrise. I could see Papa seated on a log back in the trees, a dark form framed by tall black pines and oaks. Looked a lot like this right at sunset, too, before Indian light set in, and everything melted into shadows of gray....

Fresh sunlight carved a path across the water, the tips of tiny waves flickering like struck flint. A breeze started up, curling past my ears and raising a strand of hair. My reeds whispered above my head. The water still looked dark, even though there was a mess of birds dipping for minnows and stuff on the bottom. What with wind, waves and the feeding, soon the sand would be so churned up the cove would be several shades lighter than the rest of the lake. The marsh at the mouth of the meandering creek had more mud, and held its color longer.

I'd been still so long a few little fish came up to see if the floating material around my waist was good to eat. I guess dyed cotton didn't do much for them, 'cus they darted away pretty quick. I was worried I'd startled them until I felt something larger slide by my leg–a big perch, maybe, I wasn't real good on fish. Just part of the scenery, I was, a very solid tussock....

Josh got the first duck of the day. It was quite a triumph, 'cus Wylie had just made a grab and missed. The whole flock could have shot straight up in the air over that. But Josh just stayed still and ignored all the commotion, like a good clump of weeds, and the ducks floated over his way! I found out later it took two hands for him to hang on to that duck, but somehow he kept it from breaking the surface.

Not greedy, my brother. He started floating back to shore, to hand Papa the duck. After a moment, I couldn't see him, so I wasn't sure if he'd come back out or not.

A group of wood ducks was floating my way, with some mallards and a few blue teals and ring-necked mixed in. I was surprised to see the mallards and teals–they don't dive when they can dabble–but maybe the weeds were high enough here for them. All my muscles were tightening up, in anticipation, I supposed, so I tried to calm myself.

No females. I knew my markings well enough to tell the difference, and I didn't want to risk grabbing somebody who'd left a nest for a quick snack. I could see babies bobbing with the gathering, all striped and speckled in their disguises. Surely a male would land here soon?

Maybe I could grab a male. It was nothing but trouble, the whole idea. I floated until my fingers were wrinkled and my skin starting to flare from cold, but I couldn't attract anything except females. Even the juveniles came to nibble at my weeds. Maybe my collar was *too* good.

The boys were having better luck. At least Shaw was–he had a knack for this trap. I was turned so I could watch what he was doing, and he grabbed first one blue teal and then, a few moments later, another one. That's how it's supposed to be–smooth and quiet. He made it look easy...but I didn't expect it to be easy. Wylie missed again, which made him mad, but he finally caught a fat female who wasn't smart enough to stay with the others.

I found myself wondering if she had babies, and then pushed the thought away. Made me tense up again.

Too cold...Papa was going to make me get out pretty soon, if the ducks didn't stop feeding first. I *had* to grab a duck...these classes were mostly for me, so I could stay home, instead of staying with my aunt Marta for lessons. I couldn't take up Papa's time for nothing.

Just when I was trying to talk myself into a female with no babies floating around her, two males paddled past. One was an old wood duck, the other a young mallard mix. It was like a gift from God, and I knew that I *had* to get one of them.

I didn't think–I grabbed.

Suddenly there was a heap of motion under the water, and my arms were almost jerked off. Who in creation could have guessed I'd get hold of both? Never had I held on to anything so tight–I finally understood what a death grip was like. One of the ducks panicked and kept trying to wiggle away. That one I hauled deep, so he couldn't get any air.

The other had leverage. I'd grabbed only one leg, so he was flapping wings and feet at me, trying to peck whatever had hold of him, beating at me like an enraged goose. I knew I'd be bruised, but I hung on for all I was worth; I was afraid I'd hurt his leg, see, and he'd starve if he couldn't heal. If he was gonna die from my grab, it was gonna be here and now.

Time slowed, I swear it did–the thrashing changed, no longer rhythmic, but in scattered, frenzied intervals. The wood duck had exhausted itself, and finally floated limp, but I will swear to my dying day that mallard kept moving until the last bit of air was gone from his body.

Finally there was a quiver, a little twitch along his leg, and then there wasn't any more motion.

By that time my hands were so cold I wasn't sure I *could* let go, so I didn't. Could ducks play possum? If they could, they deserved their freedom. But I had felt that mallard die...I knew I had. A lump started swelling in my throat.

Slowly I worked my way to the rocky beach, covered with a thin layer of sand myself. All I could think was that Momma would not be happy that I needed to wash my hair.

Papa met me at the waterline, nodding as he saw the birds. "I thought you got both of them. Well done, daughter."

Tears welled up and over before I could get hold of myself. Suddenly I couldn't stop shaking.

"I killed them!"

Well, you never saw such a confused bunch of boys. Josh and the others had come up to see the ducks, all full of smiles, and then their expressions sort of fell, like men whose race horse tripped at the line. That's all I saw–then my sight was too blurred to see anything.

Somebody pried the birds out of my hands (that mallard took some work–I'd made sure of him) and someone else had an arm around my shoulders. "We were supposed to, Allie!" I heard Wylie say as he hugged me. "How else could we know if we could catch dinner, if we ever needed to?" He started plucking the reeds from my disguise.

"We won't waste them, Allie," came Josh's voice from somewhere. "We'll eat them up on Sunday, honest!" He was almost pleading with me.

I couldn't talk, couldn't say I knew all that, couldn't explain worth spit. It was kinder than I'd expect them to act, what with their usual words about crybaby girls. Guess I'd proved myself enough in the past few months to merit some respect.

"We can keep the feathers, Allie, and make something beautiful from them," came Shaw's low voice. "So we always remember what a meal costs."

"Costs? These ducks were free!" Wylie said then.

The scent of Papa's tobacco and the feel of his worn chambray shirt intruded, pulling me away from the others. "You fellows get your-selves cleaned up. We'll be over there." He guided my steps to a sandy ridge. Sun had already burned away the dew–I was the only wet thing left. We sat down among the reeds, and Papa pushed his red cotton handkerchief into my hand.

I cried a bit longer, a drawn out, sobby kind of thing, and then wiped my eyes with the cloth. Papa just waited, his eyes on the lake, the light breeze lifting the fair hair laying on his collar. Warm scents of growth and decay floated in off the marsh.

"I'm sorry," I finally managed to say.

"What for? Don't ever apologize for feeling bad about killing some-thing, Allie. Taking life is a serious matter."

I tried to look at him, but my eyes kept filling with water.

"That's one reason we learn to be good with traps and weapons, daughter. So we don't make mistakes; so an animal doesn't suffer."

"I...I was afraid to let go of the mallard. I thought maybe I'd bro-ken its leg," I finally whispered.

"I'd brought my gun, in case that happened," Papa admitted. This shocked me, 'cus I hadn't noticed. Had I been so preoccupied?

We sat there awhile, the slight breeze curling round our faces. Then Papa said: "Seems like Josh and your Momma have been kill-ing our capons lately. I thought that was your job. You giving up eat-ing chicken?"

I knew what he meant. "Capon" was an old word folks used for the young male birds that would never be roosters. It surprised me that he'd noticed I'd been ducking out on wringing chicken necks. Swallowing, I tried to find an answer for him. "I felt that duck die, Papa. I felt the life drain out of its body. Chickens...well, chickens aren't good for much but eating, but they must feel it, too. Know when they're going to die, I mean."

"Not if you do a good job," he said quietly. "That's an advantage of grabbing one duck at a time. You can yank it under and break its neck." I just looked at him. "Didn't think of that, did you? That's what Shaw did. He has trouble killing, too. Think there's some of the healer strain in him. But folks gotta eat."

"Not dead things," I said quickly. "We could eat bread and potatoes and stuff."

Papa gave me a long look. "But wheat ears die so we can have bread. All those grains will never have baby wheat ears of their own, because they gave up their goodness for us. Potatoes are the roots of a living plant–a plant we kill by digging up."

Sweet lord, I'd never thought of it that way, but what's seed but thrashed wheat we've set back?

"It's a cycle, daughter. All things feed on death...and in time, we will be food. For the fire, or the worms. Our spirits go beyond, but all flesh returns to the earth."

"What about people who die wrong?" I had no idea where that question came from.

"Wrong...before their time?" I thought about his words, and then he added: "Or at the hands of the dark side, like Dolph did?"

Those tears started rising again.

"I haven't studied the mysteries as much as your aunt, Allie, so I can't swear to it, but I don't think there's anything mankind's come across yet that can kill the spirit...except maybe another man." His face grew thoughtful, and worried, suddenly. He looked quickly at me, and then back to the lake. "But that can happen when you're still living, daughter. If you kill a man, all you've done is change him from living to dead. His spirit is free, and his body returns to earth. You have to be alive to have your spirit eroded."

"So you have to eat death to have life," I murmured. It seemed that everyone, whether they had power or not, brushed up against the mysteries.

"Yes. The trick is to live well–to treat life and death with respect. Dolph didn't have much time to learn these things." There was a pause, and then Papa said slowly: "But I will tell you this, Alfreda–something I haven't told your Momma. Your brother died well. Even with the madness setting in, something human remained. He seemed to know it was time to end the chase. When he was trapped, and couldn't reach the rabbit he'd been hunting, he just turned and waited. The group came up so fast, they speared him before anyone could blink. After that, the madness set in again, so we had to kill him to save ourselves. But somehow Dolph was able to keep himself from attacking us, those few moments when he might have. I have no doubt that whatever and wherever heaven is, he's waiting for us."

That made me feel a lot better, suddenly. I wasn't sure why, but it did. "Dolph was a good person," I announced.

"True," Papa agreed.

"But sometimes he did stupid things," I went on. "Or...even mean things." I felt greatly daring, voicing that thought. "Like when he threatened to dunk me in the rain barrel if I followed him when he walked out with Becky after church."

"Folks can be mean sometimes," Papa said slowly, "and sisters and brothers can be worse than most. But when you needed each other, you stuck up for each other, didn't you?"

I nodded, not trusting myself to speak.

"Dolph was smart, and funny, and a good trapper and farmer. He was a kind son and brother, most times, and a good Catholic," Papa murmured, taking out his pouch and pipe. "He was also stubborn as a mule, and had a cutting tongue when he wished. Men need a few flaws, Allie...otherwise they might start thinking themselves perfect. Make sense?"

Guess I didn't have to worry about perfection. "Now Josh has gotta carry on for two," I muttered, repeating something Aunt Dagmar had said to Aunt Sunhild.

"No," Papa said sharply, and then seemed to work at relaxing. "Josh has gotta be himself. No one can carry another's burden. Dolph did his living and earned his rest. We need to let him go. Don't fall into that thinking, Allie. Bad enough your Momma's setting too many hopes on Joshua. Don't you do it, too."

We sat quietly for a while, the breeze pushing at us. I brushed futilely at the wet sand on my skirt while I did some thinking. Finally I said: "I'll miss the grass snakes in my bed. He always tried to pick friendly ones."

Papa started chuckling. "Good thing. Didn't you put the last one you discovered under his pillow?"

It was my turn to grin. "Yup. Wish I could tell him about being tucked behind a turtle's dream."

The flint struck iron, and Papa puffed on his pipe. "Dolph may be the safest person to tell about your lessons, Alfreda. When you say your prayers at night, it doesn't hurt to ask God to pass on that you're getting chummy with turtles and snakes. Dolph would be glad you're carrying on the tradition."

Tradition.... "Josh has been so nice to me lately, I'm not sure I can put a snake in his bed," I admitted. "If Ben would grow just a little bit more...."

This time Papa laughed aloud. Another puff, and he asked: "You going to save the feathers, like Shaw suggested?"

"What would I do with them?"

"I'll bet Shaw has some ideas."

Nodding, I slowly got to my feet. It never hurt to remember the price of something. Best to always count the cost up front. "We'd better get back and pluck those birds, or they won't hang long enough before roasting."

"Rinse off first," Papa suggested. "Or your Momma will have a fit."

I contemplated that, and repressed a grin. I could get bloody from a fall, and Momma never batted an eyelash–just patched me up. But tear my dress or muss my hair...some things never change.

A rising run of notes echoed through the woods, this time sounding like the slide of a violin. I took a deep breath, and realized I was content. It didn't matter about the bird, really...it, too, was a Mystery. And I'd know the answer in time. Everything came in its time, if you were paying attention.

Shaw walked over about then, and asked: "Do you want us to carry your ducks for you?"

I shook my head. "Thank you, but I'll carry them myself."

– END –

Author Biography

Katharine Eliska Kimbriel has held numerous traditional writer jobs (like correspondence school instructor and gold caster,) has been nominated for the Campbell, and has watched three imprints die under her feet. In other words, she's ready for success. She's published the Nuala Chronicles (SF) and Tales of Alfreda Golden-Tongue (Fantasy) as well as short fiction and nonfiction, and has written a mystery-fantasy-romance she'd like to sell.

Definitely in the works are a new Alfreda novel and a contemporary fantasy about shape shifters living in Texas. A labyrinth and herb garden framed by old roses is in the early planning stages. She is owned by two Burmese cats, shares a house with a medievalist computer geek and his marmalade cat, and works as an RMT and web wrangler during mundane times. Overall, life is good. You can stop by her live journal (she's Alfreda89) for occasional updates. Or try http://www.ke-kimbriel.com.

Artist Biography

Christopher Hershberger was born in Valdez, Alaska 4-13-1985 and started art at young age. Ever since he was three, art has always dominated his path through life. This is the first of his work that will be published and many more shall follow. Thank you for buying this book. You can contact him at christopher_hershberger@yahoo.com.

Yard Dog Press Titles As Of This Print Date

The Green Women, Laura J. Underwood
The Guardians, Lynn Abbey
Hammer Town, Selina Rosen
The Happiness Box, Beverly A. Hale
The Host Series: The Host, Fright Eater, Gang Approval, Selina Rosen
Houston, We've Got Bubbas!, Edited by Selina Rosen
How I Spent the Apocolypse, Selina Rosen
I Didn't Quite Make It To Oz, Edited by Selina Rosen
I Should Have Stayed In Oz, Edited by Selina Rosen
In the Shadows, Bradley H. Sinor
International House of Bubbas, Edited by Selina Rosen
It's the Great Bumpkin, Cletus Brown!, Katherine A. Turski
The Killswitch Review, Steven-Elliot Altman & Diane DeKelb-Rittenhouse
The Leopard's Daughter, Lee Killough
The Lightning Horse, John Moore
The Logic of Departure, Mark W. Tiedemann
The Long, Cold Walk To Mars, Jeffrey Turner
Marking the Signs and Other Tales Of Mischief, Laura J. Underwood
Material Things, Selina Rosen
Medieval Misfits: Renaissance Rejects, Tracy S. Morris
Mirror Images, Susan Satterfield
Mirror, Mirror and Other Reflections, James K. Burk
More Stories That Won't Make Your Parents Hurl, Edited by Selina Rosen
Music for Four Hands, Louis Antonelli & Edward Morris
My Life with Geeks and Freaks, Claudia Christian
The Necronomicrap: A Guide To Your Horoooscope, Tim Frayser
Playing With Secrets, Bradley H & Sue P. Sinor
Redheads In Love, Linda L. Donahue, Rhonda Eudaly, Julia S. Mandala, & Dusty Rainbolt
Reruns, Selina Rosen
Rock 'n' Roll Universe, Ken Rand
Shadows In Green, Richard Dansky
Stories That Won't Make Your Parents Hurl, Edited by Selina Rosen
Tales from Keltora, Laura J. Underwood
Tales Of the Lucky Nickel Saloon, Second Ave., Laramie, Wyoming, U S of A, Ken Rand
Tarbox Station, Rhonda Eudaly
Texistani: Indo-Pak Food From A Texas Kitchen, Beverly A. Hale
That's All Folks, J. F. Gonzalez
Through Wyoming Eyes, Ken Rand
Turn Left to Tomorrow, Robin Wayne Bailey
The Twins, Selina Rosen
Wandering Lark, Laura J. Underwood
Wings of Morning, Katharine Eliska Kimbriel

Zombies In Oz and Other Undead Musings, Robin Wayne Bailey

Double Dog
(A YDP Imprint):

#1:

Of Stars & Shadows, Mark W. Tiedemann
This Instance Of Me, Jeffrey Turner

#2:

Gods and Other Children, Bill D. Allen
Tranquility, Tracy Morris

#3:

Home Is the Hunter, James K. Burk
Farstep Station, Lazette Gifford

#4:

Sabre Dance, Melanie Fletcher
The Lunari Mask, Laura J. Underwood

#5:

House of Doors, Julia Mandala
Jaguar Moon, Linda A. Donahue

Just Cause
(A YDP Imprint):

The Bitter End
Selina Rosen

Death Under the Crescent Moon
Dusty Rainbolt

The Ghost Writer
Selina Rosen

It's Not Rocket Science: Spirituality for the Working-Class Soul
Selina Rosen

Meditations of a Hoarder
Melinda LaFevers

Not My Life
Selina Rosen

The Pit
Selina Rosen

Plots and Protagonists: A Reference Guide for Writers
Mel. White

Vanishing Fame
Selina Rosen

Non-YDP titles we distribute:

Chains of Freedom
Chains of Destruction
Jabone's Sword
Queen of Denial
Recycled
Strange Robby
Sword Masters
Selina Rosen

Three Ways to Order:

1. Write us a letter telling us what you want, then send it along with your check or money order (made payable to Yard Dog Press) to: Yard Dog Press, 710 W. Redbud Lane, Alma, AR 72921-7247

2. Contact us at selinarosen@peoplepc.com to place your order. Then send your check or money order to the address above. *This has the advantage of allowing you to check on the availability of short-stock items such as T-shirts and back-issues of Yard Dog Comics.*

3. Contact us as in #1 or #2 above and pay with a credit card or by debit from your checking account. Either give us the credit card information in your letter/Email/phone call, or go to our website and sign up for PayPal. If you send us your information, please include your name as it appears on the card, your credit card number, the expiration date, and for Discover we also need the 4-digit security code after your signature on the back. Please remember that we will include $3.00 S/H for mailing in the lower 48 states.

Watch our website at
www.yarddogpress.com
for news of upcoming projects
and new titles!!

A Note to Our Readers

We at Yard Dog Press understand that many people buy used books because they simply can't afford new ones. That said, and understanding that not everyone is made of money, we'd like you to know something that you may not have realized. Writers only make money on new books that sell. At the big houses a writer's entire future can hinge on the number of books they sell. While this isn't the case at Yard Dog Press, the honest truth is that when you sell or trade your book or let many people read it, the writer and the publishing house aren't making any money.

As much as we'd all like to believe that we can exist on love and sweet potato pie, the truth is we all need money to buy the things essential to our daily lives. Writers and publishers are no different.

We realize that these "freebies" and cheap books often turn people on to new writers and books that they wouldn't otherwise read. However we hope that you will reconsider selling your copy, and that if you trade it or let your friends borrow it, you also pass on the information that if they really like the author's work they should consider buying one of their books at full price sometime so that the writer can afford to continue to write work that entertains you.

We appreciate all our readers and *depend* upon their support.

Thanks,
The Editorial Staff
Yard Dog Press

PS – Please note that "used" books without covers have, in most cases, been stolen. Neither the author nor the publisher has made any money on these books because they were supposed to be pulped for lack of sales.

Please do not purchase books without covers.